The Story of the Tooth Fairy

The Story of the Tooth Fairy

by Tom Paxton

illustrated by Robert Sauber

MORROW JUNIOR BOOKS
New York

Watercolor and gouache were used for the full-color illustrations. The text type is 14-point Tiffany ITC.   Text copyright © 1996 by Tom Paxton
Illustrations copyright © 1996 by Robert Sauber   All rights reserved. No part of this book may be reproduced or utilized in any form or by any
means, electronic or mechanical, including photocopying, recording, or by any information storage and retrieval system, without permission in
writing from the Publisher. Inquiries should be addressed to William Morrow and Company, Inc., 1350 Avenue of the Americas, New York, NY
10019.   Printed in Hong Kong by South China Printing Company (1988) Ltd.   10   9   8   7   6   5   4   3
Library of Congress Cataloging-in-Publication Data
Paxton, Tom.   The story of the Tooth Fairy/by Tom Paxton; illustrated by Robert Sauber.   p. cm.   Summary: When seven-year-old Emily and the
fairy Glynnis exchange a tooth for a coin, the Fairy Queen announces the renewal of friendship between mortals and fairies.
ISBN 0-688-12987-0 (trade)—ISBN 0-688-12988-9 (library)   [1. Tooth Fairy—Fiction.   2. Fairies—Fiction.   3. Friendship—Fiction.]
I. Sauber, Robert, ill.   II. Title.   PZ7.P29212Sv 1996   [E]—dc20   95-13266   CIP AC

To Midge,
Jennifer,
and Kate

T.P.

To the spirit
in my life,
my wife, Suzanne

R.S.

One warm and sleepy afternoon on a day long ago a fairy child named Glynnis sat at the bottom of a garden. It was an ideal spot for her to sit in the shade and count the bees as they kissed the flowers. Fairies don't get stung by bees, and so this is the sort of job they give to the young.

"Oh!" said someone, startling the fairy child.

She looked up to see a mortal of about seven years of age, very much larger than herself.

The mortal had seen the fairy and was clearly at a loss to explain her. "Oh!" she said again.

Glynnis sprang to her feet to run. "Oh, don't go," cried the child. "I won't hurt you! But—who are you?"

"My name," said the little one, standing up straighter, "is Glynnis. And I'm a fairy," she added. "Who are you?"

"My name is Emily," said the child, "and I live up there." She pointed to a large brown house on the hill. "I don't believe in fairies," she said.

"Then how do you account for me?" asked Glynnis.

"You might be a dream I'm having," said Emily. "I might just be dreaming and you came along." She smiled, pleased with herself.

"Well, are you?" asked Glynnis. "Are you dreaming?"

"I don't think I *am* dreaming," said Emily. She pinched herself. "No, I'm sure not. Maybe," she continued, "you're something I had for lunch that didn't agree with me. My grandma says that all the time. Aren't grandmothers funny about things like that? My grandmother always says something she ate disagreed with her. Maybe you disagreed with me. Maybe you're a pickle!" Emily laughed.

"I am not a pickle," Glynnis protested, and to prove herself magical, she turned and ran up the tree trunk. She dashed out to the end of an overhanging branch, where, standing on tiptoe like a tiny ballerina, she called down, "Good-bye."

"Wait! Don't go yet!" Emily cried.

"I must," replied Glynnis. "I'm late. But if you're here tomorrow, I'll try to be here too." And just like that, she vanished.

How she managed to do it was too much for Emily to understand, for one second a fairy stood on the branch of the oak tree and the next second she was gone. For a moment Emily doubted that she'd seen the fairy; then she decided to trust herself. She'd seen a fairy all right, and her name was Glynnis, and she missed her already.

Glynnis hadn't really vanished; she had simply run down the other side of the tree trunk so quickly that Emily's eyes hadn't been able to follow her. Down the tree she ran, into a hole in another oak tree. A tunnel lay within, and the young fairy sped down its path, eager to tell the Fairy Queen of her adventure.

Out of the tunnel she raced. Before her stood a glittering
fairy castle. Once inside its open doors she hurried into a
large hall and stumbled right at the feet of Alicia, the Fairy
Queen.

Queen Alicia held out her hand. "Rise, Glynnis," she said
with a deep sigh.

Glynnis rose quickly and was about to burst out with her

tale when she saw the sorrowful expression on Queen Alicia's face. "Why are you so sad, Your Highness?" asked Glynnis.

"It's true I'm unhappy, Glynnis," said the queen. "I'm sure you know that we have had no contact with mortals for years. They used to be our companions, and we did so much for each other."

Glynnis nodded.

"The mortals have stopped thinking of us as friends, however," continued Queen Alicia. "There were some of them who spread tales that we were mischief makers and not fit to be their friends. Now they have persuaded many others to believe the worst of us. We need some mortals to think well of us if we're ever to be close to them again. I miss their companionship terribly."

"But I met a mortal this morning, Your Highness," said Glynnis.

"A mortal? She met a mortal!" whispered the other fairies. They all sat up excitedly.

"Tell me, Glynnis," commanded the queen.

Glynnis was happy to tell her everything about her short encounter with Emily. "She was lovely, Your Highness. At first she doubted me. Then she thought I was a pickle, but now I think she likes me."

Queen Alicia's eyes brightened with hope. She thought for a moment. "Return to the child, Glynnis. If what you have told us is so—if she does like you—bring us a token of your friendship. But, Glynnis," Queen Alicia continued, "you must bring a token that *only a mortal could give*. Only then will it begin to renew our friendship. Good luck, Glynnis. Now, off you go!"

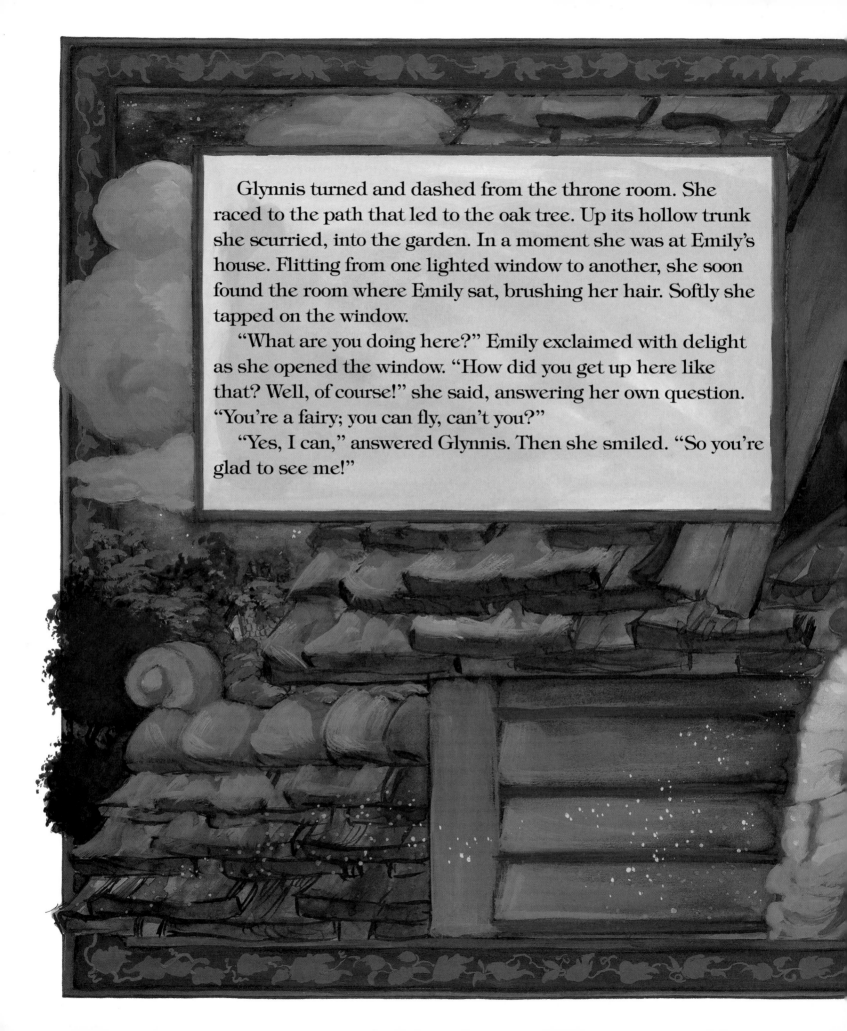

Glynnis turned and dashed from the throne room. She raced to the path that led to the oak tree. Up its hollow trunk she scurried, into the garden. In a moment she was at Emily's house. Flitting from one lighted window to another, she soon found the room where Emily sat, brushing her hair. Softly she tapped on the window.

"What are you doing here?" Emily exclaimed with delight as she opened the window. "How did you get up here like that? Well, of course!" she said, answering her own question. "You're a fairy; you can fly, can't you?"

"Yes, I can," answered Glynnis. Then she smiled. "So you're glad to see me!"

Emily looked puzzled. "Well, of course I am. We're friends, aren't we?"

"Yes!" said Glynnis, and flew once around the room. "Yes! We're friends, and we can be more. We can help bring fairies and mortals back together."

"But how can just one girl and one fairy do something like that?" asked Emily, catching Glynnis's excitement.

"Our queen says we can do it by giving each other friendship gifts," answered Glynnis, looking around Emily's room. "What kinds of things do you like? Would you like a fairy dress?"

"I would," said Emily, smiling, "but I'm a bit big, don't you think?"

"I suppose you are." Glynnis laughed. "There must be *something* I can give you in friendship, though. What other kinds of things do you like?"

"Oh, I like lots of things," Emily replied, and she proudly showed Glynnis her treasures: a plump teddy bear, a kite she flew when the weather was fine, a necklace of glass beads, and a shiny chain. The chain sparkled as it caught the light from Emily's lamp.

"That's it!" Glynnis cried. "I'll bring you something shiny! But what?"

"Well, I like all kinds of shiny things," said Emily. "Most people do."

What do we have that's shiny? wondered Glynnis. Then she brightened. "Would you like a coin? We have hundreds of coins that we're always finding but don't need. We find them in sofa cushions and behind park benches—all kinds of places."

"You don't need them? Why not?" asked Emily.

"We always have enough of everything we want, so the coins just get in the way. Would you like one?"

"I'd love one," said Emily. "I'd save it in my drawer with my necklace."

"Then that's settled," said Glynnis. "Now, what could you give me in return? Queen Alicia says it must be something that only a mortal can give." Moments passed as she tried to imagine such a gift. Suddenly Glynnis looked more closely at Emily. "Emily, you keep moving your tongue from side to side. Are you all right?"

"Oh, it's nothing," answered Emily. "It's just that I have this very loose tooth, and I know it's going to come out any minute now."

Glynnis jumped up. "A tooth! How perfect! Give me the tooth when it comes out. That will make our trade complete. I'll go back for a coin. If the tooth should come out before bedtime, leave it under your pillow, where it will be safe. I'll leave the coin in the same place."

"All right," agreed Emily.

Emily and Glynnis said good-bye, and then Glynnis disappeared from sight. Soon there was a tap on the door, and Emily's mother came in with a glass of milk and a cookie for bedtime. After her mother had left the room, Emily drank the milk and bit into the cookie. With the first bite Emily felt her loose tooth wiggle, and then it came out in her hands. Delighted, she put the tooth under her pillow and got into bed. Laying her head down, Emily wondered if she'd really get a coin.

Glynnis raced back down the tunnel to her tiny village. At the edge of the village stood a small building where the fairies put the coins they were forever finding. Glynnis threw open the door and plucked the first coin she saw. It was so new it still shone. This should do, she thought, and dashed back

up the path and into the garden. She found Emily asleep in her room. Glynnis tiptoed to her bedside. Reaching ever so carefully under the pillow, the fairy found the tooth and laid the coin there in exchange. Glynnis placed the tooth in her handkerchief and flew out the window.

Back in the underground village, Glynnis hurried to Queen Alicia.

"How did you do, Glynnis?" Queen Alicia asked.

Glynnis was happy with her good news. "I was successful, Your Highness," she said.

"She is your friend?" asked Queen Alicia.

"She is, Your Highness!" answered Glynnis. "We exchanged tokens."

"You gave her . . . ?"

"A coin, Your Highness."

The other fairies murmured expectantly.

Queen Alicia leaned forward anxiously. "And she gave you . . . ?"

"A tooth, Your Highness," answered Glynnis, unfolding her handkerchief and offering it to the queen.

"A tooth! She's brought a mortal's tooth!" shouted someone. There were cheers from the other fairies.

"You shall keep the tooth, Glynnis," said the queen, smiling broadly. "Keep it in the building where the coins now lie. When every coin is replaced with a tooth, our friendship with the mortals will be renewed, never to be broken again. From this

day forward you shall be a friend to all children, Glynnis. You shall watch them and help them. They will feel your presence, and they will tell one another about you. From now on and forever, Glynnis, you shall be known as the Tooth Fairy."

Glynnis smiled with happiness. At the same moment, Emily snuggled into her pillow with a smile of the kind that only the best dreams can bring.